To: _____

From: _____

SNOWFLAKE CITY

The Snowfarkles live in a tiny glass sphere
that sits on the mantel for most of the year.

But when it is shaken, their world fills with snow.
Read on to find out what the Snowfarkles know . . .

Published by Hallmark Gift Books,
a division of Hallmark Cards, Inc.,
Kansas City, MO 64141
Visit us on the Web at www.Hallmark.com.

Editor: Megan Langford
Art Director: Kevin Swanson
Designer and Production Artist: Bryan Ring

ISBN: 978-1-59530-418-6
1LPR7507

Printed and bound in China
JUL11

What's Shakin' in Snowflake City?

Written by Cheryl Hawkinson Illustrated by Mike Esberg

Hallmark
GIFT BOOKS

All kinds of places

have all kinds of weather,

but the weather in Snowflake

is strange altogether.

In the city of Snowflake
it doesn't just snow,
the ground shakes and rattles
while winds whip and blow.

And it happens so fast
that these storms barely last.
They whoosh in and whoosh out,
and in moments they're past.

Now, the Snowfarkle family
just waits out the shaking.
They don't even mind
when the snowflakes start flaking.

But at holiday time
there's so much to get ready,
it sure isn't helpful
when things are unsteady.

Like that night Papa Snowfarkle
climbed up a tree
and the world started wobbling,
and—oops!—so did he.

Or that day Mama Snowfarkle
stood in her kitchen
and the flour started flying
and the table was twitchin'.

Or that time when the kids
were out skating quite slickly,
and the ice shook and shivered
and cartwheeled them quickly!

Now, all the snow-grown-ups—
they don't bat an eye.
The storms come and go,
and they don't wonder why.

But some of the snow-kids
will sometimes discuss,
"How come so much snow
seems to snow down on us?"

"Are there clouds in the sky
who like clomping and stomping?

And when they start dancing
we all take a whomping?"

"Or way far away
are there mountains that grumble?

And when they get angry,
they make this place rumble?"

"Or deep underground
could there be a huge bear
who snores in his sleep
and his roars shake the air?"

Then Mama will laugh
and say "Hey, that's enough!
Where in the world
do you kids get this stuff?"

And Papa will pipe up,
"Your mother is right.
Now scurry inside—
Santa's coming tonight!

If our house shakes a bit,
and the snow swirls around,
as long as we're happy,
let those flakes tumble down!"

So the Snowfarkles gather

for games, songs, and food,

and nothing can bother

their holiday mood.

Then at last they tuck in
to dream their sweet dreams,
not knowing their city's
not quite what it seems . . .

If you liked reading about the Snowfarkles
and the crazy weather in Snowflake City,
we would love to hear from you!

Please send your comments to:
Hallmark Book Feedback
P.O. Box 419034
Mail Drop 215
Kansas City, MO 64141

Or e-mail us at:
booknotes@hallmark.com